W9-BZH-395

CANDLE TALES

by Julia Cunningham

What could they do—the cat, the mouse, the dog, the gull, the squirrel, and the pig? They had nothing in the world except the wish to give old Mr. Minikin, the candlemaker, a surprise birthday party. At the very least they needed candles and, since begging was out of the question, they intended to earn them. Not knowing how the candles were to be used, Mr. Minikin, a hard man, proposed a hard bargain. He would give one candle to each in exchange for a story, but the story must be told in verse!

The gull was first: he recited a sea-swung poem of golden treasure. And after him in the evenings that followed, each animal in turn spun his poetic tale. Mr. Minikin was delighted; and on the final night when he saw his candles, "a wondrous blaze of light and color" decorating the present from his friends, Mr. Minikin—who had never had a birthday party in his life—made a most important decision.

This touching story, like Miss Cunningham's previous one, *Macaroon,* has also been illustrated with great taste and style by Evaline Ness.

CANDLE TALES

Julia Cunningham

Illustrated by
Evaline Ness

Pantheon Books

Lighted with love for my mother

Published in New York by Pantheon Books, a division of Random House, Inc., and simultaneously in Toronto, Canada, by Random House of Canada, Limited. Manufactured in the United States of America.
Library of Congress catalog card number: 64-11879

It all began with a sigh, a sigh so loud and gusty that even the animals who lived in Mr. Minikin's woodshed heard it.

The squirrel, who was curious, spoke first: "Let's go see what the matter is."

The mouse, who was kind, agreed. And the dog and the cat and the pig followed, with the gull perched on the pig's back.

They gathered outside the low rear window of Mr. Minikin's little house and peered in. The old man was sitting hunched over his candle molds, gazing into the narrow flame that rose from a stub of wax and wick. He sighed again. "Just look at all these birthday candles," he said out loud to himself. "Twenty dozen of them in the colors of a hundred sunsets, and all for birthdays."

He looked around at his scrubby brown workroom, at the crooked bed in one corner, at the round black stove beside it, at the loppy lumpiness of his one worn easy-chair, and then back at the rows and rows of perfect candles. "I wonder what it's like to have a birthday. I just wonder."

"Oh!" breathed the mouse sorrowfully.

"Be still!" ordered the gull.

"Why?" argued the dog, plopping one ear over his right eye because he thought it made him appear tougher.

"I'm thinking, that's why!" retorted the gull. He straightened the aging feathers of his tail.

"Me too: I'm thinking," said the pig, who found it easier to repeat what others said than to invent his own sentences.

The cat raised her eyebrows toward the moon. "When pigs begin to think I shall know for sure that the moon is made of green cheese."

"No need to act so haughty," the gull commented. "The pig does the best he can."

The pig smiled at the gull gratefully.

"Besides," grinned the mouse, "maybe it is cheese."

"Let's all be still for one minute," suggested the cat. "I believe we are having the same idea."

But the squirrel couldn't wait. "And I know what it is. We'll give Mr. Minikin a birthday party!"

Small cheers arose from the pig, the cat, and the mouse, but the dog, who was practical, squashed their enthusiasm with his next remark: "How? We have no money. We only just barely get along, each of us, for ourselves. If it weren't for the town garbage I and the cat and the pig couldn't manage at all. It's not so bad for squirrels and mice and birds. You can find food in the fields and the forests. But we just can't give a party for Mr. Minikin even if he never has had one, not once, not ever."

"But we don't necessarily need food," said the cat, who was clever. "Why not just a circle of lighted candles and a song?"

"A song," murmured the pig, starting to grunt his way through "Pop Goes the Weasel."

"A song is okay," assented the dog. "That's free and all we need is breath. But candles? They cost ten cents each, even the littlest ones."

"But why buy them?" said the gull. "We can ask Mr. Minikin for some bent ones that he can't sell."

The dog laughed rudely. "Ask Mr. Minikin? We're lucky he lets us live in his shed, and if he had any use for it he wouldn't. He'd kick us out tomorrow."

"Besides," added the cat, "one doesn't beg for candles from someone whose birthday it is. That's all backwards."

The squirrel who, strangely for him, had not interrupted this discussion once, now switched his tail for attention. "Instead of standing out here in the cold night, let's ask Mr. Minikin, himself."

"You mean tell him to work out a way so that we can give him a birthday party?" said the dog, scraping his paws in the gravel with irritation.

"Don't be absurd," said the squirrel. "We tell him only that we want six candles, one for each of us, not why we want them. Then see what happens."

"I'm in favor of that," said the mouse. "He who asks not, gets not."

"Very pretty," said the cat disdainfully. "But I'm willing to try."

"Okay," said the dog doubtfully.

"Okay," repeated the pig.

"We'll see," said the retired sea gull.

So after the dog had tapped on the door of Mr. Minikin's little brown house and the old man had called "Come in!" the animals all entered and sat around the candlemaker's feet in a semicircle.

“Nice and warm in here,” said the cat, having chosen the place nearest the stove.

“You have something to say?” said Mr. Minikin grumpily. Secretly, way down inside himself, past the crusty layers of loneliness and bad temper, he was glad to have company even if it was only the scruffy animals who lived in his woodshed.

“Yes, sir,” said the mouse, “we have.” Being the youngest, the mouse paused to allow someone else to continue.

“Then speak up. What is it?”

The squirrel was about to begin when the dog stepped a paw's-length forward. "We need six candles—old ones but unlighted ones—and we aren't asking for them. We want to earn them."

"Earn, is it?" The old man's astonishment opened his eyes wide as pennies. "And how do a pig, a cat, a dog, a mouse, a squirrel, and a gull propose to earn anything, much less one of my beautiful candles?"

"That's just what we don't know," said the mouse frankly. "We're asking you."

For one small instant the old man thought of suggesting that they all come in every evening after his long day was over and just talk to him. But he was too proud to say it. They might think he was someone to feel sorry for. Also they might begin to expect small favors, like the leftover beans from his supper, or that old rug full of holes to sleep on. And that wouldn't do at all. He'd be overrun by the whole pack of them.

Then he had an idea. They wanted work? All right. He'd give it to them. And this way he would have their company at the same time. "You know any stories?"

Now it was the animals' turn to be astonished.

"Stories?" said the cat, her tail as restless as a tiger's. "Jokes, you mean?"

"Never cared for jokes," said Mr. Minikin, feeling more comfortable now that he had created a difficulty.

"Riddles?" said the squirrel. "I'm rather fond of them myself."

The dog woofed in his throat disgustedly. "Mr. Minikin said *stories*, not jokes or riddles or fiddle-dee-diddles." He turned to the old man. "You mean if we each tell you a good story we earn a candle apiece? Is that the bargain?"

"Not quite," said the candlemaker. His bargains were never just plain bargains. They were hard ones. And he felt certain that now he had gotten the best of the animals. "They have to be in poetry."

"Poetry?" said the pig. "What's that?"

The dog kicked him on the hind leg. "It's words that rhyme, like pig rhymes with dig."

"Oh, so that's poetry!" said the pig. "If I say 'Pig, dig' that's it."

"It's hopeless," said the squirrel. "Absolutely, nuttily hopeless. Even if the rest of us did manage to grind out some kind of story in verse, the pig would ruin it all."

"Maybe not," said the mouse gently. "We could help him."

The gull, who had been silent up to this moment, hopped off the pig's back onto the candlemaker's table. "Agreed, Mr. Minikin. We'll try."

"In that case," said the cat maliciously, "you may begin. The first evening is all yours."

The other animals released their breaths in relief and all stared at the gull as though this let them out of any responsibility at all.

The old gull, though his heart was beating a little too fast for his age, was a veteran of many a buffeting of wind and hard times. He faced Mr. Minikin, stood proud, beak raised, and began:

"My wings are tattered, my tail is brief,
Snipped and scattered by wind and reef,
Scraped and scratched, my feathers don't match,
And what's left of the prize I onetime was
Is a handful of fuzz and a leaf that flies—
A worn-up, torn-up leaf that flies!"

The gull puffed for a moment and then spoke again, this time with the quietness of smoke:

"Once upon a long and winter wave
And me so done I would have shaved a stone
for food,
I spied a chest. Wood it was, old wood,
Bound with tapes of thinnest brass gone green.
I latched my claws upon one edge of it
And pecked the lock, a knobbly kind of thing
That had a crown no bigger than a ring
Carved on its face. But my beak was not a key
to fit
The round, dark hole, so there was I
Perched on a box between the sea and sky.
Now I never had much in my life, but I
Had fun and freedom and one other thing—
A piece of strong and leathered, long and
weathered string!

I fetched it from my nest within the cliff,
Slipped one of the ends under and around
A strip of the brass that bound the floating chest
And like a sturdy skiff I dragged it through the
surf
And with one heave (my best) I pulled the box
aground.
All night I jabbed and poked. I crabbed and then
I joked.

I wore my claws to nubs, my temper to a stub.
I whistled, stamped, and swore and then attacked
  once more.
I thrust and dug and chewed till the splinters
  I spewed loose
Were entirely enough to stuff a goose.
At last, at dawn, I stopped, as limp as kelp,
As overdone as fish left in the sun, and added
  to the brine
A tearful that was mine. Then, just before
  I flopped
To sleep upon the beach, I reached, I touched
  the little crown
Just once and sudden—down fell the knobbly
  lock!
I lopped my wobbly head over the top and there
Instead of canned sardines were thousands of
  tiny queens
Engraved on tiny rounds as gold as any cloud!
I shouted out so loud I woke the sun straight up.

Two years I lived de luxe.
Each day I dropped a coin upon a fishing boat
And they threw back more fish than any gull
could wish.
Here be an end to words. My story tells
one thing:
All that you need for joy is air, a pair of wings
(a bird's),
And one long length of string."

There was an instant of silence. They were all smiling, even Mr. Minikin, though his smile was so lopsided it might not have been recognized as one.

"Good show!" said the dog.

The cat purred like little drums.

The squirrel thumped his tail on the floor with pleasure.

"Oink!" said the pig happily.

The mouse looked up admiringly at the gull and then said, rather shyly, "I haven't wings, or a string either, and I did all right too. Want to hear? Want to hear it now?"

"Tomorrow," said Mr. Minikin. "It is past midnight by one minute. Time we all got to bed." He looked out of the small window of chipped glass at the frosted whiteness of the grass in his tiny yard. Then he looked at the six animals. "You can sleep in here tonight, if you like," he said gruffly, "if you are quiet and don't snuffle or squeak." He turned his back on the surprised group who had never received so much as a cracker crumb from the candlemaker, much less an act of kindness.

So the gull flew to a rafter over the table. The dog stretched out in front of the stove. The mouse crept under the warmth of the dog's short tail. The cat curled up contentedly beside the stove and the pig lay down just where he was and closed his eyes.

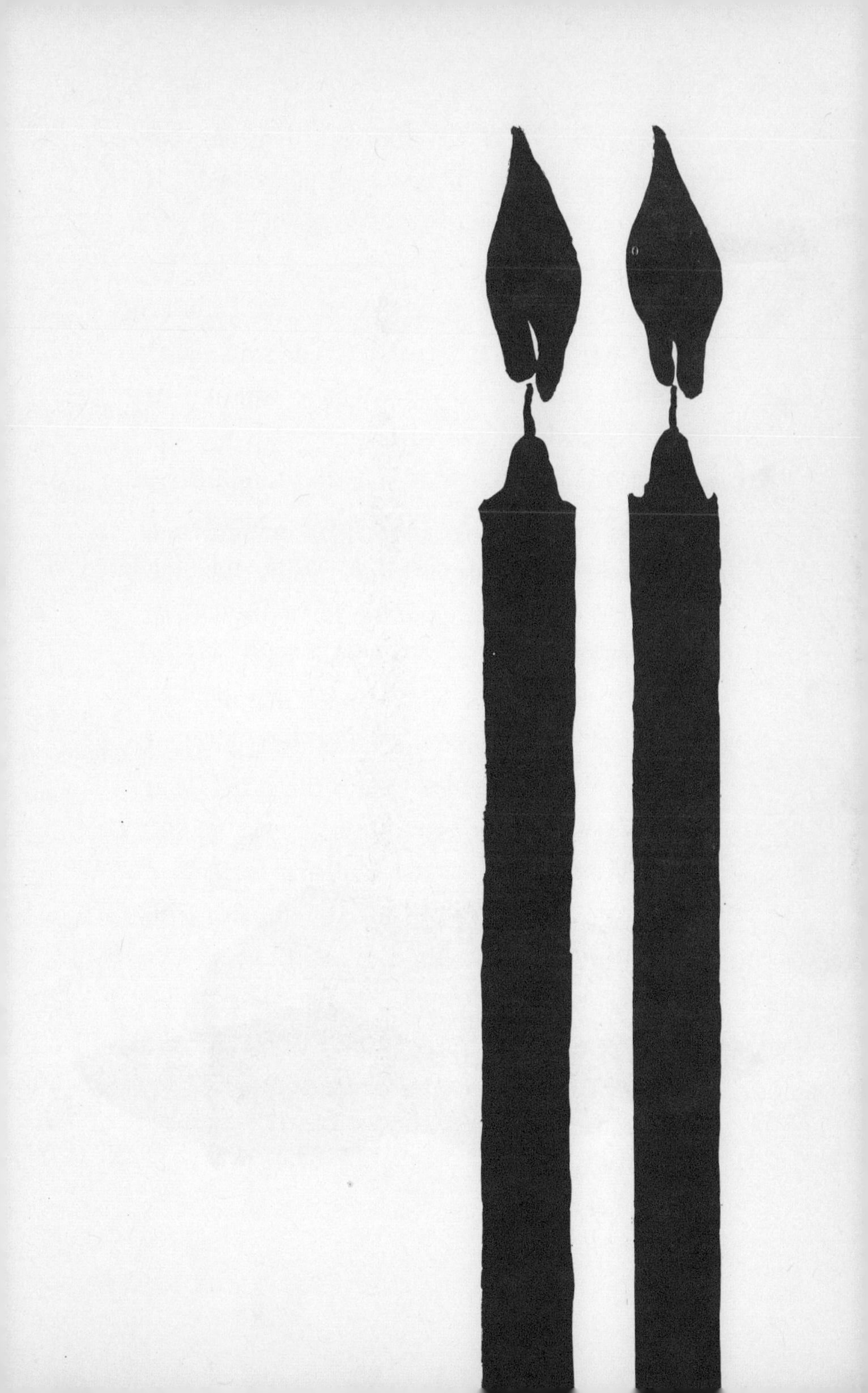

The next evening, after a day spent in woods and town, in trees and on streets, the animals filed into Mr. Minikin's cottage, glad to be indoors, and formed the same semicircle as the night before.

They all noticed the blue candle that the old man had set aside from the racks and racks of others. Mr. Minikin nodded toward the gull. "That is yours in payment for your story."

The gull, as dignified as the candlemaker, nodded solemnly back at him. But his claws tightened with pleasure on the pig's back.

The pig giggled. "You're tickling me!" he grunted.

"Now?" said the mouse. "My turn now?"

"Any time you are ready," said Mr. Minikin, leaning back in his chair.

"Well, it was like this," began the mouse. "I was playing tag with my cousin and—"

"Just a second!" said the dog. "It's supposed to be poetry."

The mouse gulped. "Oh—I completely forgot. Wait till I get my first rhyme." The wait was only as long as it takes an eye to wink.

"A mouse is commonly a quick talker,
Neat and pattery, the way he is a walker,
And me and my cousin being mice
We can talk five times to your once or twice.
Well, it was a meadowy kind of day. You know—
Bloomy in spots and flickery with leaves,
And there we lay aquiver with sun and chat,
Hats under heads, flat on our backs, counting
clouds,
When suddenly my cousin gave a squawk
And I was shocked to find him in the process
Of being carried off by a hawk.
Imagine me, small as I am, and no way at all
of following!
But I was positively, absolutely, and definitively
resolved
On a rescue and remembered that the hawk
Never dined till five.

Also I knew his address,
So if I were quick and micey, I had a chance
Of catching my cousin alive. I ran the
 underground
Of leaf and twig and log, making no sound,
Varying my speed—jog, trot, skip, and bound—
Till I arrived at his tree.
Really, I had to laugh at how easy it was
To buzz up that pine. I paused under cover
 of a cone
To see if that nasty bird was home or away.
The nest was empty except for his prey
Which consisted of my cousin, tucked away and
 weeping, tied with string.

Now if anything makes me mad it's somebody
giving somebody else
Reason to be sad. So I furiously ignored the
distress of my kin
And, after chawing through his knots,
I hurriedly made an utter mess of that black
villain's house
By severing the prop that held it to the tree
So that when he returned to flop
He would fall from the top to the bottom,
Smashing at least three bones, and just possibly
drop dead.
The two of us then swiftly skittered down
And had almost reached the roots
When a screech of rage and fury near sent
my heart to glory.
The hawk, then flying low, had seen my eyes
aglow!

He swooped and missed, retreated, then zoomed
back
To renew his attack. I yelled at him,
'Look higher! Your filthy nest's on fire!'

He swerved and alighted like a sack
Upon his home. Crack, smash! It all came
tumbling down
Like a kettle full of hash.

Cousin and I, we fled back to our meadow,
Red with triumph and a lack of breath.
No. The hawk did not meet death the moment
  that he crashed
But his eyes still flash like flints
Each time he spies the splints on both his ankle
  bones.
O, aren't I just the one, a mouse of brilliance such
As shows the brightest bright beside the
  summer's sun!"

The mouse had no sooner completed the last syllable of the last word than everyone burst out laughing. Even Mr. Minikin, whose laugh was a bit hacky from disuse, couldn't resist the happy conceit of this small creature.

"Bravo!" said the squirrel.

"Well done!" said the dog.

"Not very pure poetry," commented the cat, "but entertaining."

The animals each took up their sleeping places of the night before and more than one chuckled again in his corner as he closed his eyes.

The next evening no one stepped forward immediately from the comfortable group, though the mouse looked ready enough to take a second turn, so Mr. Minikin himself made the choice.

"How about you?" he said to the cat, who was tranquilly smoothing the fur of her long black tail.

Without haste, she gave a final lick and turned to the old man.

"As you like," she replied. For two minutes the room was silent and the cat's eyes became dreamier and dreamier. Then she began in a voice as creamy as the color of her two forepaws:

"Mine is a cushioned tale of elegance, of
nightingales
Baked in a crusty pie, of velvet chairs and gold,
Of dancing rooms and grace that falls
Like feathers everywhere you walk.

The halls were long as lanes, mirrors and
windowpanes
Gleamed with light, and flowers were changed
Every seven hours. I stalked the mansion like
a queen
And every day I dined from a silver dish
Piled with silver fish and bits of sugared toast.
I've no intent to boast because the best of cats
Often inherits less and roams the bitter roads
Of hunger and distress. But I
Was fortuned and it looked like sweet forever
Nooked as I was in such a place.

And yet there was a shadow in this light:
A vain and yellow bird, a very
Opposite of grace, a nasty old canary.
And I must firmly state that all despite
My cat's distaste for birds, I never once
Went near this one, not even just
To practice-bite outside its cage.
But, oh, what fun that little fluff
Did have in her pretended rage
To cry out 'Help!' then watch them run
Me out with brooms. Her squeaky bluff
Worked every time and soon the rooms
Where she was hung were out of bounds for cats.
The scum! But this was not enough.
One day she hit upon a way to cook
My goose for good and all. She shook
Five feathers on the floor, again
Let loose her cheeps of fear and pain.
And when they found me down the hall
Curled by a lamp, almost asleep,
They grabbed me by my lovely scruff
Without farewell or 'Sorry, friend'
And threw me out on my rear end.
Thus was I now the victim of
My gentleness and open love.

Alas, too late to speak a word
In my defense, I knew I should
Have eaten up that wicked bird
And then continued to be good."

Mr. Minikin led the applause this time. "Have you ever written poetry professionally?" he inquired.

"No," said the cat modestly, "though I have often considered doing so."

"Then do it," said the dog, who believed in action.

"Perhaps I shall," said the cat and she was so pleased she started to lick the already perfectly smooth fur of her left side.

"Nasty things, birds," said the pig ambitiously.

"I beg your pardon," said the gull.

"Beg *your* pardon," said the pig. He turned to his corner in embarrassment and closed his eyes.

"Good night," said Mr. Minikin. "Sleep well, all of you. Maybe tomorrow I might be able to prepare us all a little supper before the dog tells his story."

"My turn so soon?" said the dog. "That means I will have to think hard all day tomorrow."

Contentedly they settled down in their places and it seemed to each one of them that Mr. Minikin's little house was just beginning to feel like home.

The next evening the little supper that Mr. Minikin had been able to get together out of his not very full purse consisted of a baked potato and an apple for each animal. The cat gave her apple to the pig, and the mouse, almost the same size as the potato, only smaller, shared with the dog. But just the idea of being under a roof with something to eat cheered them all into constant smiles.

After Mr. Minikin had stacked the clean plates in the cupboard and sat down to hear the next story, it was the dog who stepped forward.

"I'm not much for poems and my grammar's
as weak
As a leek left over from the week before
Or an ant with a crutch. But here I goes.
It all began with a garbage can
And a certain flea who was fond of me.
I was rooting about for a bone or two
(And bones that winter were miserable few)
When who should appear on my left rib-side
But a flea who announced, 'I've come to reside.'
Now I've had a number of fleas in my time
Who stop to feed and then quit my hide
But never a one so impudent
As tells he's going to be permanent.
Before I could lift my leg to scratch
Him off, he said, with daring pluck,
'Leave me be and I'll bring you luck.'
'Luck, is it?' I laughed so loud
The neighborhood mongrels made a crowd.
'What's the joke?' They yapped again.
But I'm never one for making fun
Of any mite, so I sent them packing with bark
and bite.
'Now what's the angle?' I asked the flea.
'Luck for you or luck for me?'

‘Both. Just take me on. You’ll see.’
‘Okay, we’ll give it a few days’ try,’
And off we trotted, flea and I,
Hoboes under a roof of sky.
The next five days were lean except
For the flea who ate his fill and slept
And ate some more from my low supply.
It got so bad I took to the town
And walked the main street up, then down,
In search of grub. What did I meet
But occasional kicks or a boot in the legs.
But a dog who begs is a different beast
From a dog who doesn’t and a beggar I wasn’t.

At last one night I could go no more.
I crawled, done in, between a floor and a canvas
wall
And there I lay with my eyes shut tight
Not hearing or seeing the noise and light
That was right next door.
Then the flea spoke up. 'Arise,' he urged,
'And pretend you're a pup. It's a circus tent.
This is your chance. Arise and dance!'
'Dance!' I replied as I wearily eyed
The eager flea. 'Are you plumb crazy?'
'No! On your feet! I'll help you! Try!'

So I struggled up and staggered into the nearest
ring
And turned in a circle as slow as a turtle.
A child called out, 'Oh, look at the dog!'
Another cried, 'Hello, old friend!'
And, sudden, I felt a needle go in
To my thin rear end. I began to spin.
Another jab. I took a bound
And I leaped like a goat on a merry-go-round.
That blasted flea was using his ingenuity!

The music stopped and so did he.
I dropped like a log but the children yelled,
'Hip! Hip! Hooray for the dancing dog!'
A kindly clown leaned gently down
And took me to his caravan
Where he gave me milk and a half a can
Of noodle soup. And that is nearly the end of it
Except to say I was a hit
And became a star for a little bit.

But once a rover one must rove
And one day I licked my clown with love,
I shook my flea farewell and took
To the road again where the wind and rain
Sing the tune of my heart's refrain."

"What a broad and interesting life you've had," said the mouse.

"The only kind worth having," said the gull gravely.

"Oh, I don't know," said the squirrel. "Some like their worlds big and some like them small. It all depends."

"Flying's more in my line than philosophy," said the gull, closing the subject.

"You know," said the candlemaker, who had been thinking very hard while the animals talked, "these stories should be written down. I could do it on Sundays."

"How important and wonderful that sounds!" said the cat, who was fond of prominence.

"On real paper?" asked the mouse.

The dog laughed. He was tired from so much storytelling and was the first to sleep. But one by one the others followed his example and in five minutes the snug little room was full of small and peaceful breathings.

The next evening the squirrel could hardly wait for the second supper of codfish cakes and boiled potato to be over. He started to explain things even before Mr. Minikin had quite dried the last plate.

"Strictly speaking, I'm not going to tell a story at all. At least not the usual kind. I want to tell about where I live in the summertime, a little square of meadow with my birch tree in the middle."

"Get on with it then," said the gull mildly, relishing the memory of the codfish cake.

The squirrel's tail was very still and then he began to speak in a voice almost like singing:

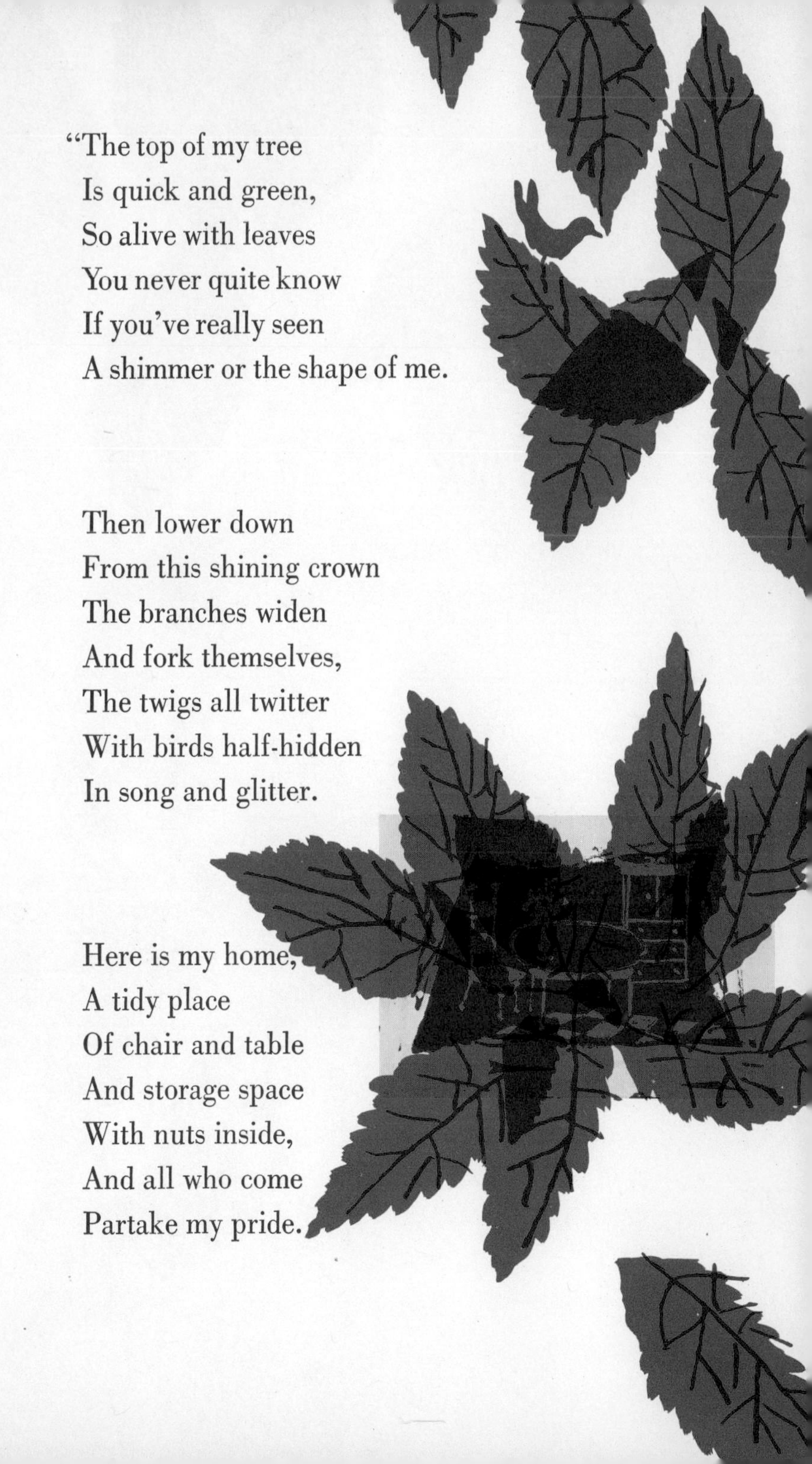

"The top of my tree
Is quick and green,
So alive with leaves
You never quite know
If you've really seen
A shimmer or the shape of me.

Then lower down
From this shining crown
The branches widen
And fork themselves,
The twigs all twitter
With birds half-hidden
In song and glitter.

Here is my home,
A tidy place
Of chair and table
And storage space
With nuts inside,
And all who come
Partake my pride.

I give them wine
In an acorn shell,
I hope they're fine
And wish them well,
I do my best
To make us shine,
Me and my nest.

Then is the ground,
A ring of grass
So soft around
The beetles pass
Through on tiptoe
Almost as though
They heard it grow.

And when I'm lazy
Here I lie,
Cushioned by daisy
And marguerite,
Sniffing the sweet
And tranquil air
That smells of sky.

I cannot say
What I give or take
Or mark one day
In this ebb and flow
From any other,
But this I know,
The world's my brother."

●

There was a very thoughtful silence all around the room as the squirrel's small summer song ended. And this time no one said anything. But the gull patted the squirrel's head with the tip of one wing and the dog licked the end of the squirrel's tail and the cat purred behind him and the pig sighed and the mouse dropped a tear on his paw and Mr. Minikin smiled very deeply.

Just before the time of the last evening all the animals had gathered for a conference with the exception of the pig, who was not invited on purpose. They knew that this dear but stupid porker would never be able to tell any kind of story, much less in verse, and not one of them wanted him to feel the hurt of his not getting a candle.

"We will have the birthday party for Mr. Minikin tonight," said the dog. "Agreed?"

"Agreed!" chorused the cat, the gull, the mouse, and the squirrel.

"You have the candles?" said the gull. "All five?"

"Yes," replied the dog. "Mr. Minikin gave them to me last night after the rest of you went to sleep.

A red one, a yellow one, a blue one, a green one, and a purple one. The cat has arranged them in a circle of moss. The squirrel has bordered the moss with acorns. The gull has dotted the center with sea shells from his own collection and the mouse has planted three tiny daisies right in the middle."

"Then you bring it in after we all are seated," suggested the squirrel to the dog.

"Right."

So it was that after the five other animals were circled around the candlemaker, the dog entered on his hind legs, carrying the wondrous blaze of light and color. As he placed it on the table before the dazed Mr. Minikin they all burst into the singing of "Happy Birthday to You!" and the pig provided a bass of rhythmic oinks.

For a moment Mr. Minikin couldn't speak or look or even think. A birthday, his first real birthday in his whole life!

Then, trying to conceal the choky feeling in his throat and the spring of tears to his eyes, he got up and pulled out of his cupboard a large platter of ten cooked turkey wings, five mackerel, seventeen roasted chestnuts, a whole cup of sunflower seeds, and a big portion of beef stew.

The singing reached the last note as they all gathered around the table and tucked into the feast. For a while only the sounds of crunching and gulping and swallowing were heard in the little house. But at last they all settled back, wiped their mouths, and just stared at the beautiful cake of moss and shells and acorns and daisies and candlelight.

"But I see only five candles," said the pig slowly. "Where is mine?"

All the animals looked at one another and then at the floor.

It was Mr. Minikin who spoke. "Did I forget yours?" he said. "I'm sorry." He pulled out the largest candle of all from his racks and it was round and proud and golden.

"But I haven't told my story yet!" said the pig.

He stood sturdily on his four stumpy legs, took a big, wheezy breath, and began:

"A pig can thrum
Like a drum."

And he stamped, *dum, dum, dum,* on the floor.

"A pig can turn
Like a churn."

And he wheeled in three circles.

"A pig can shout
Through his snout."

And he oinked twice.

"A pig can sleep
Like a sheep."

And he closed his pleasant little eyes.

"A pig is rose
To his toes."

And he stood very still to let them all see what color he was.

"A pig can mush
Through the slush."

There being no slush to mush through he smiled at everybody instead.

"A pig can toddle
With a waddle."

And he waddled a few steps and back again.

"But best a pig
Can dance a jig!"

On the word "jig" he suddenly rose on his hind legs, ears flopping, tail wiggling, his eyes alight, and went into a jig that was so gay and lively the mouse began to sing a tune to match the pig's tapping feet, the cat waved her tail like a flag, the gull hopped from leg to leg, the dog pranced around the pig, the squirrel jumped up on the pig's shoulder for the ride, and Mr. Minikin lighted the pig's golden candle with one flick of a match.

At last, ten minutes later, they all dropped, laughing, into their places.

"This is a real party!" cried the mouse.

"A truly wonderful evening," said the cat.

"More fun than anything!" said the squirrel.

"Best ever!" said the gull.

"My idea of a lark!" said the dog.

"And," said Mr. Minikin, "the most splendid birthday anyone ever had!"

He brought out a dusty bottle of dandelion punch and served each one a glassful. "Now," he said, raising his portion in a salute, "I wish to invite you all to live with me and be my friends forever."

Six cheers shook the warm little room, and though the voices were different: a squeak, a croak, a churr, a bark, a purr, and an oink, they each were saying the same thing: "God bless us all and all again, especially Mr. Minikin!"